Lightning's Feelings

 PRESS

New York • Los Angeles

Lightning is alone.
He feels lonely.

Lightning is hot.
He feels thirsty.

Lightning is trapped.
He feels scared.

Lightning is mad.
He feels angry.

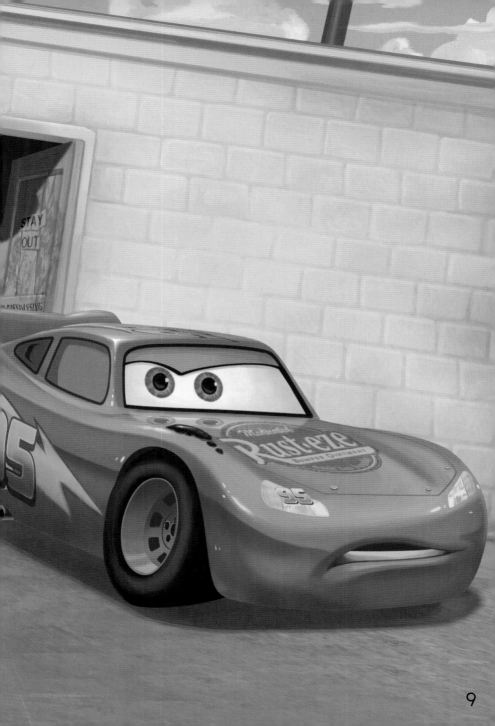

Lightning is slow.
He feels sad.

Lightning is fast.
He feels happy.

Lightning is the winner.
He feels great.
Ka-chow!

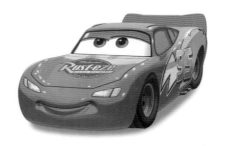